THE OLD MANSE

THE
OLD MANSE

BY

NATHANIEL HAWTHORNE

Chapman Billies
Sandwich, MA

Copyright 1904 by Houghton, Mifflin & Co.
All rights reserved

This edition published in 1997 by
Chapman Billies, Inc.
P.O. Box 819, Sandwich, MA 02563

ISBN 0-939218-00-3

NOTE

Hawthorne's *talent for descriptive writing was never exercised upon a happier theme than the Old Manse at Concord, Massachusetts. Built in 1765 by Emerson's grandfather, William, the patriot chaplain who perished early in the Revolution, the parsonage passed after his death into the hands of Dr. Ezra Ripley, who married William Emerson's widow and succeeded him in the pastorate. It is still in the possession of the Ripley family. At three different periods it was the temporary home of Ralph Waldo Emerson, who wrote his 'Nature' in the small back room upon the second story, looking out upon the river,*

Note

the North Bridge, and the battlefield. When Hawthorne married Sophia Peabody in July, 1842, they took up their abode in the Old Manse, which had stood vacant since the death of Dr. Ripley. Here they passed three years of idyllic happiness. Their first child was born in the Old Manse, and here were written many of the well-known pieces included in the collection entitled 'Mosses from an Old Manse.' The ancient homestead fascinated the imagination both of Hawthorne and his wife, and there are many passages in their letters and journals describing the Eden-like surroundings of the new Adam and Eve, as the happy young couple loved to call themselves. When Hawthorne came to write an introductory paper for his 'Mosses,' he gath-

Note

ered these impressions into one of the most perfect of his descriptive essays. It is this essay which is reprinted here.

B. P.

4 PARK STREET.

THE OLD MANSE

THE OLD MANSE

Between two tall gateposts of rough-hewn stone (the gate itself having fallen from its hinges at some unknown epoch) we beheld the gray front of the old parsonage terminating the vista of an avenue of black ash-trees. It was now a twelve-month since the funeral procession of the venerable clergyman, its last inhabitant, had turned from that gateway towards the village burying-ground. The wheel-track leading to the door, as well as the whole breadth of the avenue, was almost overgrown with grass, affording dainty mouthfuls to two or three vagrant cows and an old white horse who had his own

The Old Manse

living to pick up along the roadside. The glimmering shadows that lay half asleep between the door of the house and the public highway were a kind of spiritual medium, seen through which the edifice had not quite the aspect of belonging to the material world. Certainly it had little in common with those ordinary abodes which stand so imminent upon the road that every passer-by can thrust his head, as it were, into the domestic circle. From these quiet windows the figures of passing travellers looked too remote and dim to disturb the sense of privacy. In its near retirement and accessible seclusion it was the very spot for the residence of a clergyman, — a man not estranged from human life, yet en-

The Old Manse

veloped in the midst of it with a veil woven of intermingled gloom and brightness. It was worthy to have been one of the time-honored parsonages of England in which, through many generations, a succession of holy occupants pass from youth to age, and bequeath each an inheritance of sanctity to pervade the house and hover over it as with an atmosphere.

Nor, in truth, had the Old Manse ever been profaned by a lay occupant until that memorable summer afternoon when I entered it as my home. A priest had built it; a priest had succeeded to it; other priestly men from time to time had dwelt in it; and children born in its chambers had grown up to assume the

The Old Manse

priestly character. It was awful to reflect how many sermons must have been written there. The latest inhabitant alone — he by whose translation to paradise the dwelling was left vacant — had penned nearly three thousand discourses, besides the better, if not the greater, number that gushed living from his lips. How often, no doubt, had he paced to and fro along the avenue, attuning his meditations to the sighs and gentle murmurs, and deep and solemn peals of the wind among the lofty tops of the trees! In that variety of natural utterances he could find something accordant with every passage of his sermon, were it of tenderness or reverential fear. The boughs over my head seemed shad-

The Old Manse

owy with solemn thoughts as well as with rustling leaves. I took shame to myself for having been so long a writer of idle stories, and ventured to hope that wisdom would descend upon me with the falling leaves of the avenue, and that I should light upon an intellectual treasure in the Old Manse well worth those hoards of long-hidden gold which people seek for in moss-grown houses. Profound treatises of morality; a layman's unprofessional and therefore unprejudiced views of religion; histories (such as Bancroft might have written had he taken up his abode here as he once proposed) bright with picture, gleaming over a depth of philosophic thought,— these were the works that might fitly have

The Old Manse

flowed from such a retirement. In the humblest event I resolved at least to achieve a novel that should evolve some deep lesson and should possess physical substance enough to stand alone.

In furtherance of my design, and as if to leave me no pretext for not fulfilling it, there was in the rear of the house the most delightful little nook of a study that ever afforded its snug seclusion to a scholar. It was here that Emerson wrote *Nature;* for he was then an inhabitant of the Manse, and used to watch the Assyrian dawn and Paphian sunset and moonrise from the summit of our eastern hill. When I first saw the room its walls were blackened with the smoke of unnumbered

The Old Manse

years, and made still blacker by the grim prints of Puritan ministers that hung around. These worthies looked strangely like bad angels, or at least like men who had wrestled so continually and so sternly with the devil that somewhat of his sooty fierceness had been imparted to their own visages. They had all vanished now; a cheerful coat of paint and golden tinted paper-hangings lighted up the small apartment; while the shadow of a willow-tree that swept against the overhanging eaves attempered the cheery western sunshine. In place of the grim prints there was the sweet and lovely head of one of Raphael's Madonnas, and two pleasant little pictures of the Lake of Como. The only other deco-

The Old Manse

rations were a purple vase of flowers, always fresh, and a bronze one containing graceful ferns. My books (few, and by no means choice; for they were chiefly such waifs as chance had thrown in my way) stood in order about the room, seldom to be disturbed.

The study had three windows, set with little, old-fashioned panes of glass, each with a crack across it. The two on the western side looked, or rather peeped, between the willow branches down into the orchard, with glimpses of the river through the trees. The third, facing northward, commanded a broader view of the river at a spot where its hitherto obscure waters gleam forth into the light of history. It was at this

The Old Manse

window that the clergyman who then dwelt in the Manse stood watching the outbreak of a long and deadly struggle between two nations; he saw the irregular array of his parishioners on the farther side of the river and the glittering line of the British on the hither bank. He awaited in an agony of suspense the rattle of the musketry. It came, and there needed but a gentle wind to sweep the battle smoke around this quiet house.

Perhaps the reader, whom I cannot help considering as my guest in the Old Manse and entitled to all courtesy in the way of sight-showing,— perhaps he will choose to take a nearer view of the memorable spot. We stand now on the river's

The Old Manse

brink. It may well be called the Concord, the river of peace and quietness; for it is certainly the most unexcitable and sluggish stream that ever loitered imperceptibly towards its eternity — the sea. Positively, I had lived three weeks beside it before it grew quite clear to my perception which way the current flowed. It never has a vivacious aspect except when a northwestern breeze is vexing its surface on a sunshiny day. From the incurable indolence of its nature, the stream is happily incapable of becoming the slave of human ingenuity, as is the fate of so many a wild, free mountain torrent. While all things else are compelled to subserve some useful purpose, it idles its sluggish life

The Old Manse

away in lazy liberty, without turning a solitary spindle or affording even water-power enough to grind the corn that grows upon its banks. The torpor of its movement allows it nowhere a bright, pebbly shore, nor so much as a narrow strip of glistening sand, in any part of its course. It slumbers between broad prairies, kissing the long meadow grass, and bathes the overhanging boughs of elder bushes and willows or the roots of elms and ash-trees and clumps of maples. Flags and rushes grow along its plashy shore; the yellow water-lily spreads its broad, flat leaves on the margin; and the fragrant white pond-lily abounds, generally selecting a position just so far from the river's

The Old Manse

brink that it cannot be grasped save at the hazard of plunging in.

It is a marvel whence this perfect flower derives its loveliness and perfume, springing as it does from the black mud over which the river sleeps, and where lurk the slimy eel and speckled frog and the mud turtle, whom continual washing cannot cleanse. It is the very same black mud out of which the yellow lily sucks its obscene life and noisome odor. Thus we see, too, in the world that some persons assimilate only what is ugly and evil from the same moral circumstances which supply good and beautiful results — the fragrance of celestial flowers — to the daily life of others.

The reader must not, from any

The Old Manse

testimony of mine, contract a dislike towards our slumberous stream. In the light of a calm and golden sunset it becomes lovely beyond expression; the more lovely for the quietude that so well accords with the hour, when even the wind, after blustering all day long, usually hushes itself to rest. Each tree and rock, and every blade of grass, is distinctly imaged, and, however unsightly in reality, assumes ideal beauty in the reflection. The minutest things of earth and the broad aspect of the firmament are pictured equally without effort and with the same felicity of success. All the sky glows downward at our feet; the rich clouds float through the unruffled bosom of the stream like heavenly thoughts

The Old Manse

through a peaceful heart. We will not, then, malign our river as gross and impure while it can glorify itself with so adequate a picture of the heaven that broods above it; or, if we remember its tawny hue and the muddiness of its bed, let it be a symbol that the earthliest human soul has an infinite spiritual capacity and may contain the better world within its depths. But, indeed, the same lesson might be drawn out of any mud puddle in the streets of a city; and, being taught us everywhere, it must be true.

Come, we have pursued a somewhat devious track in our walk to the battle-ground. Here we are, at the point where the river was crossed by the old bridge, the possession of

The Old Manse

which was the immediate object of the contest. On the hither side grow two or three elms, throwing a wide circumference of shade, but which must have been planted at some period within the threescore years and ten that have passed since the battle day. On the farther shore, overhung by a clump of elder bushes, we discern the stone abutment of the bridge. Looking down into the river, I once discovered some heavy fragments of the timbers, all green with half a century's growth of water moss; for during that length of time the tramp of horses and human footsteps has ceased along this ancient highway. The stream has here about the breadth of twenty strokes of a swimmer's arm, — a

The Old Manse

space not too wide when the bullets were whistling across. Old people who dwell hereabouts will point out the very spots on the western bank where our countrymen fell down and died; and on this side of the river an obelisk of granite has grown up from the soil that was fertilized with British blood. The monument, not more than twenty feet in height, is such as it befitted the inhabitants of a village to erect in illustration of a matter of local interest rather than what was suitable to commemorate an epoch of national history. Still, by the fathers of the village this famous deed was done; and their descendants might rightfully claim the privilege of building a memorial.

The Old Manse

A humbler token of the fight, yet a more interesting one than the granite obelisk, may be seen close under the stone wall which separates the battle-ground from the precincts of the parsonage. It is the grave — marked by a small, moss-grown fragment of stone at the head and another at the foot — the grave of two British soldiers who were slain in the skirmish, and have ever since slept peacefully where Zechariah Brown and Thomas Davis buried them. Soon was their warfare ended; a weary night march from Boston, a rattling volley of musketry across the river, and then these many years of rest. In the long procession of slain invaders who passed into eternity from the battle-

The Old Manse

fields of the revolution, these two nameless soldiers led the way.

Lowell, the poet, as we were once standing over this grave, told me a tradition in reference to one of the inhabitants below. The story has something deeply impressive, though its circumstances cannot altogether be reconciled with probability. A youth in the service of the clergyman happened to be chopping wood, that April morning, at the back door of the Manse, and when the noise of battle rang from side to side of the bridge he hastened across the intervening field to see what might be going forward. It is rather strange, by the way, that this lad should have been so diligently at work when the whole population of town and coun-

The Old Manse

try were startled out of their customary business by the advance of the British troops. Be that as it might, the tradition says that the lad now left his task and hurried to the battlefield with the axe still in his hand. The British had by this time retreated, the Americans were in pursuit; and the late scene of strife was thus deserted by both parties. Two soldiers lay on the ground—one was a corpse; but, as the young New Englander drew nigh, the other Briton raised himself painfully upon his hands and knees and gave a ghastly stare into his face. The boy,—it must have been a nervous impulse, without purpose, without thought, and betokening a sensitive and impressible nature rather than a hardened one, — the

The Old Manse

boy uplifted his axe and dealt the wounded soldier a fierce and fatal blow upon the head.

I could wish that the grave might be opened; for I would fain know whether either of the skeleton soldiers has the mark of an axe in his skull. The story comes home to me like truth. Oftentimes, as an intellectual and moral exercise, I have sought to follow that poor youth through his subsequent career, and observe how his soul was tortured by the blood stain, contracted as it had been before the long custom of war had robbed human life of its sanctity, and while it still seemed murderous to slay a brother man. This one circumstance has borne more fruit for me than all that history tells us of the fight.

The Old Manse

Many strangers come in the summer time to view the battle-ground. For my own part, I have never found my imagination much excited by this or any other scene of historic celebrity; nor would the placid margin of the river have lost any of its charm for me had men never fought and died there. There is a wilder interest in the tract of land — perhaps a hundred yards in breadth — which extends between the battlefield and the northern face of our Old Manse, with its contiguous avenue and orchard. Here, in some unknown age, before the white man came, stood an Indian village, convenient to the river, whence its inhabitants must have drawn so large a part of their subsistence. The site

The Old Manse

is identified by the spear and arrow heads, the chisels, and other implements of war, labor, and the chase, which the plough turns up from the soil. You see a splinter of stone, half hidden beneath a sod; it looks like nothing worthy of note; but, if you have faith enough to pick it up, behold a relic! Thoreau, who has a strange faculty of finding what the Indians have left behind them, first set me on the search; and I afterwards enriched myself with some very perfect specimens, so rudely wrought that it seemed almost as if chance had fashioned them. Their great charm consists in this rudeness and in the individuality of each article, so different from the productions of civilized machinery, which shapes

The Old Manse

everything on one pattern. There is exquisite delight, too, in picking up for one's self an arrowhead that was dropped centuries ago and has never been handled since, and which we thus receive directly from the hand of the red hunter, who purposed to shoot it at his game or at an enemy. Such an incident builds up again the Indian village and its encircling forest, and recalls to life the painted chiefs and warriors, the squaws at their household toil, and the children sporting among the wigwams, while the little wind-rocked pappoose swings from the branch of the tree. It can hardly be told whether it is a joy or a pain, after such a momentary vision, to gaze around in the broad daylight of reality and

The Old Manse

see stone fences, white houses, potato fields, and men doggedly hoeing in their shirt-sleeves and homespun pantaloons. But this is nonsense. The Old Manse is better than a thousand wigwams.

The Old Manse! We had almost forgotten it, but will return thither through the orchard. This was set out by the last clergyman, in the decline of his life, when the neighbors laughed at the hoary-headed man for planting trees from which he could have no prospect of gathering fruit. Even had that been the case, there was only so much the better motive for planting them, in the pure and unselfish hope of benefiting his successors, —an end so seldom achieved by more ambitious efforts. But the

The Old Manse

old minister, before reaching his patriarchal age of ninety, ate the apples from this orchard during many years, and added silver and gold to his annual stipend by disposing of the superfluity. It is pleasant to think of him walking among the trees in the quiet afternoons of early autumn and picking up here and there a windfall, while he observes how heavily the branches are weighed down, and computes the number of empty flour barrels that will be filled by their burden. He loved each tree, doubtless, as if it had been his own child. An orchard has a relation to mankind, and readily connects itself with matters of the heart. The trees possess a domestic character ; they have lost

The Old Manse

the wild nature of their forest kindred, and have grown humanized by receiving the care of man as well as by contributing to his wants. There is so much individuality of character, too, among apple-trees that it gives them an additional claim to be the objects of human interest. One is harsh and crabbed in its manifestations; another gives us fruit as mild as charity. One is churlish and illiberal, evidently grudging the few apples that it bears; another exhausts itself in free-hearted benevolence. The variety of grotesque shapes into which apple-trees contort themselves has its effect on those who get acquainted with them: they stretch out their crooked branches, and take such hold of the imagination that we

The Old Manse

remember them as humorists and odd-fellows. And what is more melancholy than the old apple-trees that linger about the spot where once stood a homestead, but where there is now only a ruined chimney rising out of a grassy and weed-grown cellar? They offer their fruit to every wayfarer, — apples that are bitter sweet with the moral of Time's vicissitude.

I have met with no other such pleasant trouble in the world as that of finding myself, with only the two or three mouths which it was my privilege to feed, the sole inheritor of the old clergyman's wealth of fruits. Throughout the summer there were cherries and currants; and then came autumn, with his im-

The Old Manse

mense burden of apples, dropping them continually from his overladen shoulders as he trudged along. In the stillest afternoon, if I listened, the thump of a great apple was audible, falling without a breath of wind, from the mere necessity of perfect ripeness. And, besides, there were pear-trees, that flung down bushels upon bushels of heavy pears; and peach-trees, which, in a good year, tormented me with peaches, neither to be eaten nor kept, nor, without labor and perplexity, to be given away. The idea of an infinite generosity and exhaustless bounty on the part of our Mother Nature was well worth obtaining through such cares as these. That feeling can be enjoyed in perfection only by the natives of

The Old Manse

summer islands, where the breadfruit, the cocoa, the palm, and the orange grow spontaneously and hold forth the ever-ready meal ; but likewise almost as well by a man long habituated to city life, who plunges into such a solitude as that of the Old Manse, where he plucks the fruit of trees that he did not plant, and which therefore, to my heterodox taste, bear the closest resemblance to those that grew in Eden. It has been an apothegm these five thousand years, that toil sweetens the bread it earns. For my part (speaking from hard experience, acquired while belaboring the rugged furrows of Brook Farm), I relish best the free gifts of Providence.

Not that it can be disputed that

The Old Manse

the light toil requisite to cultivate a moderately-sized garden imparts such zest to kitchen vegetables as is never found in those of the market gardener. Childless men, if they would know something of the bliss of paternity, should plant a seed, — be it squash, bean, Indian corn, or perhaps a mere flower or worthless weed, — should plant it with their own hands, and nurse it from infancy to maturity altogether by their own care. If there be not too many of them, each individual plant becomes an object of separate interest. My garden, that skirted the avenue of the Manse, was of precisely the right extent. An hour or two of morning labor was all that it required. But I used to visit and revisit it a dozen

The Old Manse

times a day, and stand in deep contemplation over my vegetable progeny with a love that nobody could share or conceive of who had never taken part in the process of creation. It was one of the most bewitching sights in the world to observe a hill of beans thrusting aside the soil, or a row of early peas just peeping forth sufficiently to trace a line of delicate green. Later in the season the humming-birds were attracted by the blossoms of a peculiar variety of bean; and they were a joy to me, those little spiritual visitants, for deigning to sip airy food out of my nectar cups. Multitudes of bees used to bury themselves in the yellow blossoms of the summer squashes. This, too, was a deep satisfaction;

The Old Manse

although when they had laden themselves with sweets they flew away to some unknown hive, which would give back nothing in requital of what my garden had contributed. But I was glad thus to fling a benefaction upon the passing breeze with a certainty that somebody must profit by it, and that there would be a little more honey in the world to allay the sourness and bitterness which mankind is always complaining of. Yes, indeed; my life was the sweeter for that honey.

Speaking of summer squashes, I must say a word of their beautiful and varied forms. They presented an endless diversity of urns and vases, shallow or deep, scalloped or plain, moulded in patterns which a sculptor

The Old Manse

would do well to copy, since Art has never invented anything more graceful. A hundred squashes in the garden were worthy, in my eyes at least, of being rendered indestructible in marble. If ever Providence (but I know it never will) should assign me a superfluity of gold, part of it shall be expended for a service of plate, or most delicate porcelain, to be wrought into the shapes of summer squashes gathered from vines which I will plant with my own hands. As dishes for containing vegetables they would be peculiarly appropriate.

But not merely the squeamish love of the beautiful was gratified by my toil in the kitchen garden. There was a hearty enjoyment, likewise, in

The Old Manse

observing the growth of the crook-necked winter squashes, from the first little bulb, with the withered blossom adhering to it, until they lay strewn upon the soil, big, round fellows, hiding their heads beneath the leaves, but turning up their great yellow rotundities to the noontide sun. Gazing at them, I felt that by my agency something worth living for had been done. A new substance was born into the world. They were real and tangible existences, which the mind could seize hold of and rejoice in. A cabbage, too, — especially the early Dutch cabbage, which swells to a monstrous circumference, until its ambitious heart often bursts asunder, — is a matter to be proud of when we

The Old Manse

can claim a share with the earth and sky in producing it. But, after all, the hugest pleasure is reserved until these vegetable children of ours are smoking on the table, and we, like Saturn, make a meal of them.

What with the river, the battlefield, the orchard and the garden, the reader begins to despair of finding his way back into the Old Manse. But in agreeable weather it is the truest hospitality to keep him out-of-doors. I never grew quite acquainted with my habitation till a long spell of sulky rain had confined me beneath its roof. There could not be a more sombre aspect of external Nature than as then seen from the windows of my study. The great willow-tree had caught and

The Old Manse

retained among its leaves a whole cataract of water, to be shaken down at intervals by the frequent gusts of wind. All day long, and for a week together, the rain was drip-drip-dripping and splash-splash-splashing from the eaves, and bubbling and foaming into the tubs beneath the spouts. The old, unpainted shingles of the house and out-buildings were black with moisture; and the mosses of ancient growth upon the walls looked green and fresh, as if they were the newest things and afterthought of Time. The usually mirrored surface of the river was blurred by an infinity of raindrops; the whole landscape had a completely water-soaked appearance, conveying the impression that the

The Old Manse

earth was wet through like a sponge; while the summit of a wooded hill, about a mile distant, was enveloped in a dense mist, where the demon of the tempest seemed to have his abiding-place and to be plotting still direr inclemencies.

Nature has no kindness, no hospitality, during a rain. In the fiercest heat of sunny days she retains a secret mercy, and welcomes the wayfarer to shady nooks of the woods whither the sun cannot penetrate; but she provides no shelter against her storms. It makes us shiver to think of those deep, umbrageous recesses, those overshadowing banks, where we found such enjoyment during the sultry afternoons. Not a twig of foliage there but would dash

The Old Manse

a little shower into our faces. Looking reproachfully towards the impenetrable sky, — if sky there be above that dismal uniformity of cloud, — we are apt to murmur against the whole system of the universe, since it involves the extinction of so many summer days in so short a life by the hissing and sputtering rain. In such spells of weather — and it is to be supposed such weather came — Eve's bower in paradise must have been but a cheerless and aguish kind of shelter, nowise comparable to the old parsonage, which had resources of its own to beguile the week's imprisonment. The idea of sleeping on a couch of wet roses!

Happy the man who in a rainy day can betake himself to a huge

The Old Manse

garret, stored, like that of the Manse, with lumber that each generation has left behind it from a period before the revolution. Our garret was an arched hall, dimly illuminated through small and dusty windows; it was but a twilight at the best; and there were nooks, or rather caverns, of deep obscurity, the secrets of which I never learned, being too reverent of their dust and cobwebs. The beams and rafters, roughly hewn and with strips of bark still on them, and the rude masonry of the chimneys, made the garret look wild and uncivilized, — an aspect unlike what was seen elsewhere in the quiet and decorous old house. But on one side there was a little whitewashed apartment which bore the traditionary

The Old Manse

title of the Saint's Chamber, because holy men in their youth had slept and studied and prayed there. With its elevated retirement, its one window, its small fireplace, and its closet, convenient for an oratory, it was the very spot where a young man might inspire himself with solemn enthusiasm and cherish saintly dreams. The occupants, at various epochs, had left brief records and ejaculations inscribed upon the walls. There, too, hung a tattered and shrivelled roll of canvas, which on inspection proved to be the forcibly wrought picture of a clergyman, in wig, band, and gown, holding a Bible in his hand. As I turned his face towards the light he eyed me with an air of authority such as men of

The Old Manse

his profession seldom assume in our days. The original had been pastor of the parish more than a century ago, a friend of Whitefield, and almost his equal in fervid eloquence. I bowed before the effigy of the dignified divine, and felt as if I had now met face to face with the ghost by whom, as there was reason to apprehend, the Manse was haunted.

Houses of any antiquity in New England are so invariably possessed with spirits that the matter seems hardly worth alluding to. Our ghost used to heave deep sighs in a particular corner of the parlor, and sometimes rustled paper, as if he were turning over a sermon in the long upper entry, — where nevertheless he was invisible in spite of the bright

The Old Manse

moonshine that fell through the eastern window. Not improbably he wished me to edit and publish a selection from a chest full of manuscript discourses that stood in the garret. Once, while Hillard and other friends sat talking with us in the twilight, there came a rustling noise as of a minister's silk gown, sweeping through the very midst of the company so closely as almost to brush against the chairs. Still there was nothing visible. A yet stranger business was that of a ghostly servant maid, who used to be heard in the kitchen at deepest midnight, grinding coffee, cooking, ironing, — performing, in short, all kinds of domestic labor, — although no traces of anything accomplished could be

The Old Manse

detected the next morning. Some neglected duty of her servitude — some ill-starched ministerial band — disturbed the poor damsel in her grave and kept her at work without any wages.

But to return from this digression. A part of my predecessor's library was stored in the garret, — no unfit receptacle indeed for such dreary trash as comprised the greater number of volumes. The old books would have been worth nothing at an auction. In this venerable garret, however, they possessed an interest, quite apart from their literary value, as heirlooms, many of which had been transmitted down through a series of consecrated hands from the days of the mighty Puritan divines.

The Old Manse

Autographs of famous names were to be seen in faded ink on some of their flyleaves; and there were marginal observations or interpolated pages closely covered with manuscript in illegible shorthand, perhaps concealing matter of profound truth and wisdom. The world will never be the better for it. A few of the books were Latin folios, written by Catholic authors; others demolished Papistry, as with a sledge-hammer, in plain English. A dissertation on the book of Job — which only Job himself could have had patience to read — filled at least a score of small, thickset quartos, at the rate of two or three volumes to a chapter. Then there was a vast folio body of divinity — too corpulent a

The Old Manse

body, it might be feared, to comprehend the spiritual element of religion. Volumes of this form dated back two hundred years or more, and were generally bound in black leather, exhibiting precisely such an appearance as we should attribute to books of enchantment. Others equally antique were of a size proper to be carried in the large waistcoat pockets of old times, — diminutive, but as black as their bulkier brethren, and abundantly interfused with Greek and Latin quotations. These little old volumes impressed me as if they had been intended for very large ones, but had been unfortunately blighted at an early stage of their growth.

The rain pattered upon the roof

The Old Manse

and the sky gloomed through the dusty garret windows, while I burrowed among these venerable books in search of any living thought which should burn like a coal of fire, or glow like an inextinguishable gem, beneath the dead trumpery that had long hidden it. But I found no such treasure; all was dead alike; and I could not but muse deeply and wonderingly upon the humiliating fact that the works of man's intellect decay like those of his hands. Thought grows mouldy. What was good and nourishing food for the spirits of one generation affords no sustenance for the next. Books of religion, however, cannot be considered a fair test of the enduring and vivacious properties of human

The Old Manse

thought, because such books so seldom really touch upon their ostensible subject, and have, therefore, so little business to be written at all. So long as an unlettered soul can attain to saving grace, there would seem to be no deadly error in holding theological libraries to be accumulations of, for the most part, stupendous impertinence.

Many of the books had accrued in the latter years of the last clergyman's lifetime. These threatened to be of even less interest than the elder works, a century hence, to any curious inquirer who should then rummage them as I was doing now. Volumes of the " Liberal Preacher " and " Christian Examiner," occasional sermons, controversial pam-

The Old Manse

phlets, tracts, and other productions of a like fugitive nature took the place of the thick and heavy volumes of past time. In a physical point of view there was much the same difference as between a feather and a lump of lead; but, intellectually regarded, the specific gravity of old and new was about upon a par. Both also were alike frigid. The elder books, nevertheless, seemed to have been earnestly written, and might be conceived to have possessed warmth at some former period; although, with the lapse of time, the heated masses had cooled down even to the freezing point. The frigidity of the modern productions, on the other hand, was characteristic and inherent, and evidently had little to

The Old Manse

do with the writer's qualities of mind and heart. In fine, of this whole dusty heap of literature I tossed aside all the sacred part, and felt myself none the less a Christian for eschewing it. There appeared no hope of either mounting to the better world on a Gothic staircase of ancient folios or of flying thither on the wings of a modern tract.

Nothing, strange to say, retained any sap except what had been written for the passing day and year without the remotest pretension or idea of permanence. There were a few old newspapers, and still older almanacs, which reproduced to my mental eye the epochs when they had issued from the press, with a distinctness that was altogether unaccountable. It was as if I had found bits of magic looking-glass among the books, with the images of a vanished century in them. I turned my eyes towards the tattered picture above mentioned, and asked of the austere divine wherefore it was that he and his brethren, after the most painful rummaging and groping into their minds, had been able to produce nothing half so real as these newspaper scribblers and almanac makers had thrown off in the effervescence of a moment. The portrait responded not ; so I sought an answer for myself. It is the age itself that writes newspapers and almanacs, which, therefore, have a distinct purpose and meaning at the time, and a kind of intelligible truth for all times ;

The Old Manse

whereas most other works — being written by men who, in the very act, set themselves apart from their age — are likely to possess little significance when new, and none at all when old. Genius, indeed, melts many ages into one, and thus effects something permanent, yet still with a similarity of office to that of the more ephemeral writer. A work of genius is but the newspaper of a century, or perchance of a hundred centuries.

Lightly as I have spoken of these old books, there yet lingers with me a superstitious reverence for literature of all kinds. A bound volume has a charm in my eyes similar to what scraps of manuscript possess for the good Mussulman. He ima-

The Old Manse

gines that those wind-wafted records are perhaps hallowed by some sacred verse ; and I, that every new book or antique one may contain the " open sesame," — the spell to disclose treasures hidden in some unsuspected cave of Truth. Thus it was not without sadness that I turned away from the library of the Old Manse.

Blessed was the sunshine when it came again at the close of another stormy day, beaming from the edge of the western horizon ; while the massive firmament of clouds threw down all the gloom it could, but served only to kindle the golden light into a more brilliant glow by the strongly contrasted shadows. Heaven smiled at the earth, so long

The Old Manse

unseen, from beneath its heavy eyelid. To-morrow for the hill-tops and the wood-paths.

Or it might be that Ellery Channing came up the avenue to join me in a fishing excursion on the river. Strange and happy times were those when we cast aside all irksome forms and strait-laced habitudes, and delivered ourselves up to the free air, to live like the Indians or any less conventional race during one bright semicircle of the sun. Rowing our boat against the current, between wide meadows, we turned aside into the Assabeth. A more lovely stream than this, for a mile above its junction with the Concord, has never flowed on earth, — nowhere, indeed, except to lave the interior regions of a

The Old Manse

poet's imagination. It is sheltered from the breeze by woods and a hill-side; so that elsewhere there might be a hurricane, and here scarcely a ripple across the shaded water. The current lingers along so gently that the mere force of the boatman's will seems sufficient to propel his craft against it. It comes flowing softly through the midmost privacy and deepest heart of a wood which whispers it to be quiet; while the stream whispers back again from its sedgy borders, as if river and wood were hushing one another to sleep. Yes; the river sleeps along its course and dreams of the sky and of the clustering foliage, amid which fall showers of broken sunlight, imparting specks of vivid cheerfulness, in contrast with the quiet depth of the

The Old Manse

prevailing tint. Of all this scene, the slumbering river has a dream picture in its bosom. Which, after all, was the most real—the picture, or the original?—the objects palpable to our grosser senses, or their apotheosis in the stream beneath? Surely the disembodied images stand in closer relation to the soul. But both the original and the reflection had here an ideal charm, and, had it been a thought more wild, I could have fancied that this river had strayed forth out of the rich scenery of my companion's inner world; only the vegetation along its banks should then have had an Oriental character.

Gentle and unobtrusive as the river is, yet the tranquil woods seem hardly satisfied to allow it passage.

The Old Manse

The trees are rooted on the very verge of the water, and dip their pendent branches into it. At one spot there is a lofty bank, on the slope of which grow some hemlocks, declining across the stream with outstretched arms, as if resolute to take the plunge. In other places the banks are almost on a level with the water; so that the quiet congregation of trees set their feet in the flood, and are fringed with foliage down to the surface. Cardinal flowers kindle their spiral flames and illuminate the dark nooks among the shrubbery. The pond-lily grows abundantly along the margin — that delicious flower, which, as Thoreau tells me, opens its virgin bosom to the first sunlight and perfects its be-

The Old Manse

ing through the magic of that genial kiss. He has beheld beds of them unfolding in due succession as the sunrise stole gradually from flower to flower — a sight not to be hoped for unless when a poet adjusts his inward eye to a proper focus with the outward organ. Grape-vines here and there twine themselves around shrub and tree and hang their clusters over the water within reach of the boatman's hand. Oftentimes they unite two trees of alien race in an inextricable twine, marrying the hemlock and the maple against their will, and enriching them with a purple offspring of which neither is the parent. One of these ambitious parasites has climbed into the upper branches of a tall white pine, and is

The Old Manse

still ascending from bough to bough, unsatisfied till it shall crown the tree's airy summit with a wreath of its broad foliage and a cluster of its grapes.

The winding course of the stream continually shut out the scene behind us, and revealed as calm and lovely a one before. We glided from depth to depth, and breathed new seclusion at every turn. The shy kingfisher flew from the withered branch close at hand to another at a distance, uttering a shrill cry of anger or alarm. Ducks that had been floating there since the preceding eve were startled at our approach, and skimmed along the glassy river, breaking its dark surface with a bright streak. The pickerel leaped

The Old Manse

from among the lily-pads. The turtle, sunning itself upon a rock or at the root of a tree, slid suddenly into the water with a plunge. The painted Indian who paddled his canoe along the Assabeth three hundred years ago could hardly have seen a wilder gentleness displayed upon its banks and reflected in its bosom than we did. Nor could the same Indian have prepared his noontide meal with more simplicity. We drew up our skiff at some point where the overarching shade formed a natural bower, and there kindled a fire with the pine cones and decayed branches that lay strewn plentifully around. Soon the smoke ascended among the trees, impregnated with a savory incense, not heavy, dull, and surfeiting, like the

The Old Manse

steam of cookery within doors, but sprightly and piquant. The smell of our feast was akin to the woodland odors with which it mingled : there was no sacrilege committed by our intrusion there : the sacred solitude was hospitable, and granted us free leave to cook and eat in the recess that was at once our kitchen and banqueting hall. It is strange what humble offices may be performed in a beautiful scene without destroying its poetry. Our fire, red gleaming among the trees, and we beside it, busied with culinary rites and spreading out our meal on a moss-grown log, all seemed in unison with the river gliding by and the foliage rustling over us. And, what was strangest, neither did our

The Old Manse

mirth seem to disturb the propriety of the solemn woods; although the hobgoblins of the old wilderness and the will-of-the-wisps that glimmered in the marshy places might have come trooping to share our table talk, and have added their shrill laughter to our merriment. It was the very spot in which to utter the extremest nonsense or the profoundest wisdom, or that ethereal product of the mind which partakes of both, and may become one or the other, in correspondence with the faith and insight of the auditor.

So amid sunshine and shadow, rustling leaves and sighing waters, up gushed our talk like the babble of a fountain. The evanescent spray was Ellery's; and his, too, the lumps

The Old Manse

of golden thought that lay glimmering in the fountain's bed and brightened both our faces by the reflection. Could he have drawn out that virgin gold and stamped it with the mint mark that alone gives currency, the world might have had the profit, and he the fame. My mind was the richer merely by the knowledge that it was there. But the chief profit of those wild days to him and me lay, not in any definite idea, not in any angular or rounded truth, which we dug out of the shapeless mass of problematical stuff, but in the freedom which we thereby won from all custom and conventionalism and fettering influences of man on man. We were so free to-day that it was impossible to be slaves again

The Old Manse

to-morrow. When we crossed the threshold of the house or trod the thronged pavements of a city, still the leaves of the trees that overhang the Assabeth were whispering to us, "Be free! be free!" Therefore along that shady river-bank there are spots, marked with a heap of ashes and half-consumed brands, only less sacred in my remembrance than the hearth of a household fire.

And yet how sweet, as we floated homeward adown the golden river at sunset,— how sweet was it to return within the system of human society, not as to a dungeon and a chain, but as to a stately edifice, whence we could go forth at will into statelier simplicity! How gently, too, did the sight of the Old Manse,

The Old Manse

best seen from the river, overshadowed with its willow and all environed about with the foliage of its orchard and avenue, — how gently did its gray, homely aspect rebuke the speculative extravagances of the day! It had grown sacred in connection with the artificial life against which we inveighed ; it had been a home for many years in spite of all; it was my home too ; and, with these thoughts, it seemed to me that all the artifice and conventionalism of life was but an impalpable thinness upon its surface, and that the depth below was none the worse for it. Once, as we turned our boat to the bank, there was a cloud, in the shape of an immensely gigantic figure of a hound, couched above the house,

The Old Manse

as if keeping guard over it. Gazing at this symbol, I prayed that the upper influences might long protect the institutions that had grown out of the heart of mankind.

If ever my readers should decide to give up civilized life, cities, houses, and whatever moral or material enormities in addition to these the perverted ingenuity of our race has contrived, let it be in the early autumn. Then Nature will love him better than at any other season, and will take him to her bosom with a more motherly tenderness. I could scarcely endure the roof of the old house above me in those first autumnal days. How early in the summer, too, the prophecy of autumn comes! Earlier in some years

The Old Manse

than in others; sometimes even in the first weeks of July. There is no other feeling like what is caused by this faint, doubtful, yet real perception — if it be not rather a foreboding — of the year's decay, so blessedly sweet and sad in the same breath.

Did I say that there was no feeling like it? Ah, but there is a half-acknowledged melancholy like to this when we stand in the perfected vigor of our life and feel that Time has now given us all his flowers, and that the next work of his never idle fingers must be to steal them one by one away.

I have forgotten whether the song of the cricket be not as early a token of autumn's approach as any other,

The Old Manse

— that song which may be called an audible stillness; for though very loud and heard afar, yet the mind does not take note of it as a sound, so completely is its individual existence merged among the accompanying characteristics of the season. Alas for the pleasant summer time! In August the grass is still verdant on the hills and in the valleys; the foliage of the trees is as dense as ever, and as green; the flowers gleam forth in richer abundance along the margin of the river, and by the stone walls, and deep among the woods; the days, too, are as fervid now as they were a month ago; and yet in every breath of wind and in every beam of sunshine we hear the whispered farewell and behold the part-

The Old Manse

ing smile of a dear friend. There is a coolness amid all the heat, a mildness in the blazing noon. Not a breeze can stir but it thrills us with the breath of autumn. A pensive glory is seen in the far golden gleams, among the shadows of the trees. The flowers—even the brightest of them, and they are the most gorgeous of the year—have this gentle sadness wedded to their pomp, and typify the character of the delicious time each within itself. The brilliant cardinal flower has never seemed gay to me.

Still later in the season Nature's tenderness waxes stronger. It is impossible not to be fond of our mother now; for she is so fond of us! At other periods she does not make

The Old Manse

this impression on me, or only at rare intervals; but in those genial days of autumn, when she has perfected her harvests and accomplished every needful thing that was given her to do, then she overflows with a blessed superfluity of love. She has leisure to caress her children now. It is good to be alive at such times. Thank Heaven for breath — yes, for mere breath — when it is made up of a heavenly breeze like this! It comes with a real kiss upon our cheeks; it would linger fondly around us if it might; but, since it must be gone, it embraces us with its whole kindly heart and passes onward to embrace likewise the next thing that it meets. A blessing is flung abroad and scattered far and wide over the earth, to be gathered up by all who choose. I recline upon the still unwithered grass and whisper to myself, "O perfect day! O beautiful world! O beneficent God!" And it is the promise of a blessed eternity; for our Creator would never have made such lovely days and have given us the deep hearts to enjoy them, above and beyond all thought, unless we were meant to be immortal. This sunshine is the golden pledge thereof. It beams through the gates of paradise and shows us glimpses far inward.

By and by, in a little time, the outward world puts on a drear austerity. On some October morning there is a heavy hoar-frost on the grass and along the tops of the fences;

The Old Manse

and at sunrise the leaves fall from the trees of our avenue without a breath of wind, quietly descending by their own weight. All summer long they have murmured like the noise of waters; they have roared loudly while the branches were wrestling with the thunder gust; they have made music both glad and solemn; they have attuned my thoughts by their quiet sound as I paced to and fro beneath the arch of intermingling boughs. Now they can only rustle under my feet. Henceforth the gray parsonage begins to assume a larger importance, and draws to its fireside, — for the abomination of the air-tight stove is reserved till wintry weather, — draws closer and closer to its fireside the vagrant impulses that had

The Old Manse

gone wandering about through the summer.

When summer was dead and buried the Old Manse became as lonely as a hermitage. Not that ever — in my time at least — it had been thronged with company; but, at no rare intervals, we welcomed some friend out of the dusty glare and tumult of the world, and rejoiced to share with him the transparent obscurity that was floating over us. In one respect our precincts were like the Enchanted Ground through which the pilgrim travelled on his way to the Celestial City! The guests, each and all, felt a slumberous influence upon them; they fell asleep in chairs, or took a more deliberate siesta on the sofa, or were

The Old Manse

seen stretched among the shadows of the orchard, looking up dreamily through the boughs. They could not have paid a more acceptable compliment to my abode, nor to my own qualities as a host. I held it as a proof that they left their cares behind them as they passed between the stone gate-posts at the entrance of our avenue, and that the so powerful opiate was the abundance of peace and quiet within and all around us. Others could give them pleasure and amusement or instruction — these could be picked up anywhere; but it was for me to give them rest — rest in a life of trouble. What better could be done for those weary and world-worn spirits? — for him whose career of perpetual action was

The Old Manse

impeded and harassed by the rarest of his powers and the richest of his acquirements? — for another who had thrown his ardent heart from earliest youth into the strife of politics, and now, perchance, began to suspect that one lifetime is too brief for the accomplishment of any lofty aim? — for her on whose feminine nature had been imposed the heavy gift of intellectual power, such as a strong man might have staggered under, and with it the necessity to act upon the world? — in a word, not to multiply instances, what better could be done for anybody who came within our magic circle than to throw the spell of a tranquil spirit over him? And when it had wrought its full effect, then we

The Old Manse

dismissed him, with but misty reminiscences, as if he had been dreaming of us.

Were I to adopt a pet idea, as so many people do, and fondle it in my embraces to the exclusion of all others, it would be, that the great want which mankind labors under at this present period is sleep. The world should recline its vast head on the first convenient pillow and take an age-long nap. It has gone distracted through a morbid activity, and, while preternaturally wide awake, is nevertheless tormented by visions that seem real to it now, but would assume their true aspect and character were all things once set right by an interval of sound repose. This is the only method of getting rid

The Old Manse

of old delusions and avoiding new ones; of regenerating our race, so that it might in due time awake as an infant out of dewy slumber; of restoring to us the simple perception of what is right, and the single-hearted desire to achieve it, both of which have long been lost in consequence of this weary activity of brain and torpor or passion of the heart that now afflict the universe. Stimulants, the only mode of treatment hitherto attempted, cannot quell the disease; they do but heighten the delirium.

Let not the above paragraph ever be quoted against the author; for, though tinctured with its modicum of truth, it is the result and expression of what he knew, while he was writing, to be but a distorted survey of

The Old Manse

the state and prospects of mankind. There were circumstances around me which made it difficult to view the world precisely as it exists; for, severe and sober as was the Old Manse, it was necessary to go but a little way beyond its threshold before meeting with stranger moral shapes of men than might have been encountered elsewhere in a circuit of a thousand miles.

These hobgoblins of flesh and blood were attracted thither by the widespreading influence of a great original thinker, who had his earthly abode at the opposite extremity of our village. His mind acted upon other minds of a certain constitution with wonderful magnetism, and drew many men upon long pilgrimages to

The Old Manse

speak with him face to face. Young visionaries — to whom just so much of insight had been imparted as to make life all a labyrinth around them — came to seek the clew that should guide them out of their self-involved bewilderment. Grayheaded theorists — whose systems, at first air, had finally imprisoned them in an iron frame-work — travelled painfully to his door, not to ask deliverance, but to invite the free spirit into their own thraldom. People that had lighted on a new thought, or a thought that they fancied new, came to Emerson, as the finder of a glittering gem hastens to a lapidary, to ascertain its quality and value. Uncertain, troubled, earnest wanderers through the midnight of the moral world be-

The Old Manse

held his intellectual fire as a beacon burning on a hill-top, and, climbing the difficult ascent, looked forth into the surrounding obscurity more hopefully than hitherto. The light revealed objects unseen before, — mountains, gleaming lakes, glimpses of a creation among the chaos; but, also, as was unavoidable, it attracted bats and owls and the whole host of night birds, which flapped their dusky wings against the gazer's eyes, and sometimes were mistaken for fowls of angelic feather. Such delusions always hover nigh whenever a beacon fire of truth is kindled.

For myself, there had been epochs of my life when I, too, might have asked of this prophet the master word that should solve me the riddle of the

The Old Manse

universe ; but now, being happy, I felt as if there were no question to be put, and therefore admired Emerson as a poet of deep beauty and austere tenderness, but sought nothing from him as a philosopher. It was good, nevertheless, to meet him in the woodpaths, or sometimes in our avenue, with that pure intellectual gleam diffused about his presence like the garment of a shining one; and he so quiet, so simple, so without pretension, encountering each man alive as if expecting to receive more than he could impart. And, in truth, the heart of many an ordinary man had, perchance, inscriptions which he could not read. But it was impossible to dwell in his vicinity without inhaling more or less the

The Old Manse

mountain atmosphere of his lofty thought, which, in the brains of some people, wrought a singular giddiness, — new truth being as heady as new wine. Never was a poor little country village infested with such a variety of queer, strangely-dressed, oddly-behaved mortals, most of whom took upon themselves to be important agents of the world's destiny, yet were simply bores of a very intense water. Such, I imagine, is the invariable character of persons who crowd so closely about an original thinker as to draw in his unuttered breath and thus become imbued with a false originality. This triteness of novelty is enough to make any man of common sense blaspheme at all ideas of less than a century's stand-

The Old Manse

ing, and pray that the world may be petrified and rendered immovable in precisely the worst moral and physical state that it ever yet arrived at, rather than be benefited by such schemes of such philosophers.

And now I begin to feel — and perhaps should have sooner felt — that we have talked enough of the Old Manse. Mine honored reader, it may be, will vilify the poor author as an egotist for babbling through so many pages about a moss-grown country parsonage, and his life within its walls and on the river and in the woods, and the influences that wrought upon him from all these sources. My conscience, however, does not reproach me with betraying anything too sacredly individual

The Old Manse

to be revealed by a human spirit to its brother or sister spirit. How narrow—how shallow and scanty too—is the stream of thought that has been flowing from my pen, compared with the broad tide of dim emotions, ideas, and associations which swell around me from that portion of my existence! How little have I told! and of that little, how almost nothing is even tinctured with any quality that makes it exclusively my own! Has the reader gone wandering, hand in hand with me, through the inner passages of my being? and have we groped together into all its chambers and examined their treasures or their rubbish? Not so. We have been standing on the greensward, but just within the cavern's mouth, where the

The Old Manse

common sunshine is free to penetrate, and where every footstep is therefore free to come. I have appealed to no sentiment or sensibilities save such as are diffused among us all. So far as I am a man of really individual attributes, I veil my face; nor am I, nor have I ever been, one of those supremely hospitable people who serve up their own hearts, delicately fried, with brain sauce, as a tidbit for their beloved public.

Glancing back over what I have written, it seems but the scattered reminiscences of a single summer. In fairyland there is no measurement of time; and, in a spot so sheltered from the turmoil of life's ocean, three years hastened away with a noiseless flight, as the breezy sunshine

The Old Manse

chases the cloud shadows across the depths of a still valley. Now came hints, growing more and more distinct, that the owner of the old house was pining for his native air. Carpenters next appeared, making a tremendous racket among the outbuildings, strewing the green grass with pine shavings and chips of chestnut joists, and vexing the whole antiquity of the place with their discordant renovations. Soon, moreover, they divested our abode of the veil of woodbine which had crept over a large portion of its southern face. All the aged mosses were cleared unsparingly away; and there were horrible whispers about brushing up the external walls with a coat of paint — a purpose as little to my taste

The Old Manse

as might be that of rouging the venerable cheeks of one's grandmother. But the hand that renovates is always more sacrilegious than that which destroys. In fine, we gathered up our household goods, drank a farewell cup of tea in our pleasant little breakfast room,—delicately fragrant tea, an unpurchasable luxury, one of the many angel gifts that had fallen like dew upon us,— and passed forth between the tall stone gateposts as uncertain as the wandering Arabs where our tent might next be pitched. Providence took me by the hand, and — an oddity of dispensation which, I trust, there is no irreverence in smiling at—has led me, as the newspapers announce while I am writing, from the Old Manse into a custom

The Old Manse

house. As a story teller, I have often contrived strange vicissitudes for my imaginary personages, but none like this.

*　　*　　*　　*　　*　　*

FINIS